Sometimes

Sometimes

Keith Baker

Green Light Readers
Harcourt, Inc.

Orlando   Austin   New York
San Diego   Toronto   London

Sometimes I am happy.

Sometimes I am sad.

I like who I am.

I like what I do.

Sometimes I am hot.

Sometimes I am cold.

I like who I am.

I like what I do.

Sometimes I am up.

Sometimes I am down.

I like who I am.

I like what I do.

Sometimes I am red.

Sometimes I am blue.

I'm all of these things.
What about you?

Do you sometimes wish to be different?
Who or what would you like to be?
Make a mask to show your family and friends!

Mask Yourself

1 Draw and cut out your mask.

2 Glue it to a paper plate.

3 Tape a Popsicle stick to the back.

- **paper plate**
- **paper**
- **scissors**
- **glue**
- **crayons or markers**
- **Popsicle stick**
- **tape**

Hold the mask in front of your face. Act like your mask!

Meet the Author-Illustrator

Dear Boys and Girls,
My favorite color is green because I was born on St. Patrick's Day. When I was a boy, I loved to swim and ride my bike, just like the alligator in the story!

I still like to swim and ride my bike. I also like to work in my garden and cook. And, of course, I like to draw and paint. I really DO like what I do!

Keith Baker